T0196231

Touched by an Angel

Jada A. Smith

authorHOUSE®

AuthorHouse™
1663 Liberty Drive
Bloomington, IN 47403
www.authorhouse.com
Phone: 1-800-839-8640

First published by AuthorHouse 7/29/2011

ISBN: 978-1-4634-3372-7 (sc)
ISBN: 978-1-4634-3371-0 (e)

Library of Congress Control Number: 2011911287

Printed in the United States of America

Any people depicted in stock imagery provided by Thinkstock are models, and such images are being used for illustrative purposes only. Certain stock imagery © Thinkstock.

This book is printed on acid-free paper.

The Touched By An Angel
series was created by

Cover design by

*To those who did not turn away from
God during times of trouble and to those who
did, may you find your way back to Him.*

Chapter 1

**Keep thy tongue from evil, and thy
lips from speaking guile.**

-Psalm 34:13

In the kitchen, sixteen-year-old, Tracy stood at the stove frying chicken legs on a skillet. Her feet were sore from the ten mile hike home. Her skin, usually a hazel tone and soft, was now pale and rough. Her big brown eyes, usually sparkling and shining with contentment, had become dull and fogged with grief. Exhaustion crept over them, as she could scarcely keep them open. As Tracy dabbed the greasy fried chicken legs with a white paper towel, she heard the front door open and close.

"You're late." Tracy snapped as her younger brother Jeremiah walked into the kitchen, "the street lights came on an hour ago."

"Relax T; I'm here now ain't I?" Jeremiah shot back as he took a seat at the round kitchen table. Tracy glared at her thirteen-year-old brother. She knew that he was still hurting from the incident but his attitude was getting way out of hand.

"Seriously Miah, what could you and those boys possibly be doing this time of night." Tracy said ignoring the smart comment. Jeremiah just shrugged his shoulders.

"We do guy stuff." He said.

"Guy stuff huh?" Tracy repeated as she carried the platter of fried chicken to the table.

"Don't think too much of it." Jeremiah said as he fixed the cap on his head.

"Miah, don't get mixed up with those boys." Tracy told him, snatching the cap off his head. "They're nothing but trouble."

"They're my friends, T." He said; seizing his cap back. "Ain't nothin' you can do about it."

"Who do you think you are?" Tracy snapped banging her fists on the table.

"You can't boss me around." Jeremiah snapped back standing up from the table. "You ain't mama."

"I'm your older sister and like it or not, I'm responsible for you until mama gets home." Tracy shouted, "What? Do you think I like taking care of you?"

"I didn't ask you to." Jeremiah shouted, "I can take care of myself."

"Then go ahead," Tracy screamed, "when you fall flat on your back don't look to me to help you up. For goodness sake Miah, sometimes I wish you were never born." Tracy slapped her hand over her mouth. "What did I do?" she asked herself.

"Miah, I-"

"I wish you weren't my sister." Jeremiah hollered before Tracy could finish. Jeremiah raced to his bedroom and slammed the door shut. Tracy sat stunned. Her face felt hot and she couldn't move. She dug her face into her hands and cried.

Chapter 2

**...weeping may endure for a night, but
joy cometh in the morning.**

-Psalm 30:5

Jeremiah lay across his bed. His heart was pounding and his head raced as he fought the urge to cry.

"Only babies cry." He told himself. Jeremiah sat up on his bed and pulled off his sneakers. They were white and stainless when his father had bought them for him but now they were creased and splattered with different shades of brown. The laces were soggy and weak. None the less, Jeremiah loved them. He glanced at a picture that sat framed on his nightstand. In the picture his father laid in green grass with his hands behind his head, smiling. Their mother laid her head on his stomach, laughing. The picture had been taken a year ago but Jeremiah remembered it like it was yesterday.

It was a beautiful summer afternoon at the park. Jeremiah was twelve and Tracy, fifteen. The sun was shining brightly and the temperature was at a boil.

"Ay pops," Jeremiah called out to his father, "go long!"

"Throw the ball, Miah!" his father called out, his arms waving high in the air. Jeremiah smiled and tightly gripped his light brown fingers around the laces of the football, like his father had taught him too. He looked down at his new white sneakers he'd gotten, as an early birthday present from his father, that morning. He threw the ball hard and far. He watched his father run and catch the ball while toppling to the ground.

"Pops, you ok?" Jeremiah asked running over to his father's aid.

"Just fine, just fine;" His father replied getting up from the ground.

"Baby, you alright?" mama asked getting up from the picnic table.

"I'm fine dear," his father answered. "T!" He called to his daughter.

"Yes daddy?" Tracy said looking up from her book.

"Are you still the fastest runner on that ol' track team?" her father teased.

"If you say so daddy;" Tracy said.

"Aw, you still can't beat me. Shoot, I'd run circles around you." He said.

"I wouldn't bet on it if I were you." Tracy said smiling.

"I'll prove it to you." He said. "First one to the oak tree wins."

"It's ok daddy." Tracy teased, "I wouldn't want to embarrass you in front of your wife." Jeremiah, now sitting on the picnic table, snickered. Their mother smiled.

"Come on, T." Her father ordered pulling her up from the table.

"Daddy!" Tracy whined.

"Ready?" her father said. "On your mark, get set...go."

"Good times," Jeremiah thought. Of course Tracy had beaten their father. Tracy was the fastest runner in town. Jeremiah lay across his bed. He took a deep breath and let it out. His life hadn't been the same since his father died, since his father was killed. Jeremiah looked up at an article that was taped to his wall.

4

"Top Policeman Shot and Stabbed to Death." His daddy had been the top policeman on the force and was shot while on an undercover case. Some crook was robbing banks and stashing all the loot somewhere underground. The crook was caught and had a life sentence but to Jeremiah his father was the real one who had to pay the price. Sometimes when he dreams, Jeremiah can see the crook's face; dark and scary looking, smeared with his father's blood, holding a bloody blade, his cruel voice whispering that he was next. Jeremiah wiped the tears from dark brown eyes as the telephone started to ring.

"Hello?" Jeremiah said into the receiver.

"Hey, we're going out." A voice familiar to Jeremiah said. Jeremiah paused before answering. He put the phone down and tipped-toed into hall way to see if Tracy was around. She wasn't. She was nowhere in sight. Jeremiah went back into the bedroom and held the phone back to his ear.

"I'll meet ya'll in 10 minutes." He said.

"Good. Wait till you see what I got." Jeremiah heard the voice say, then nothing but a dial tone.

Chapter 3

For the Lord himself shall descend from heaven with a shout, with the voice of the archangel, and with the trump of God: and the dead in Christ shall rise first:

-1 Thessalonians 4:16

Tracy ran quickly down the street. Her heart burned, her sides ached and her feet begged her to stop but she couldn't. Tracy knew it was late and she didn't care, she had to see him. She came to a sudden stop. She looked up at the giant thick metal gate and pushed it open. Tracy walked slowly up the stone path, passing by the tombstones. She took deep breaths inhaling the thick time air. The moon and the stars lit up the silky black sky. The crickets and the owls played a sweet, calming harmony. Tracy soon came across a certain tombstone. She kneeled beside it as she fingered the engraved letters; R.I.P Jackson Nimrod. Tears rolled down her cheeks as she tried to find the strength to speak.

"Hi daddy." She whispered; brushing the lose strands of her black hair out of her face. "How's life up there in heaven?" She sniffled as she wiped her face with the back of her hand.

"Is it anything like you ever imagined?" She spoke again. Her lips curved up into somewhat of a smile. "I bet it is and more."

"Daddy I need you." Tracy said as her throat filled with tears. "We all do." And there Tracy sat spilling her guts to her father's spirit. She told him everything.

"Mama's working three jobs now, daddy. Miah's all screwed up with the wrong people and I don't what to do anymore." Tracy said.

"Only an angel can help us now." She said quietly. A random small gust of wind came through. Tracy closed her eyes as the air wrapped its self around her. It seemed to caress her. Her heart was filled with warmth. She smiled as a single tear fell from her eye and just like that the wind vanished. Tracy leaned in and pressed her lips against the piece of stone.

"I love you, daddy." Tracy spoke softly as she kissed her dad goodnight.

Chapter 4

The Lord knoweth how to deliver the godly out of temptations, and to reserve the unjust unto the day of judgment to be punished:

- II Peter 2:9

Jeremiah walked up the block. The streetlights were shinning bright and the atmosphere was quiet. It was chilly. He rubbed his hands together wishing he had worn a jacket. He took a left into an alley behind Gold Wood Middle School, where he attended. There he met up with some of his boys.

"Eh Miah," greeted Theodore, a fifteen-year-old boy with tight dark brown braids and possessive brown eyes.

"Hey Theo," Jeremiah replied as they tapped knuckles. "What's up ya'll?!" He said acknowledging the other eight boys. Jeremiah look over in the corner of the alley where he saw a boy named Dennis passed out on top of a pile of garbage bags. Dennis was a light skinned brother, with hazel eyes and brown curly white boy hair, always mistaken for a white boy but was mixed with both soul food and wonder bread.

"Ay yo, what's up with Denny?" Jeremiah asked Theo.

"D? Man, he's higher than a cloud in the sky." Theo chuckled.

"High? Off of what?"

"Wait till you see what Calvin has." Theo said with a devilish smile on his face.

Chapter 5

For every one that asketh receiveth; and he that seeketh findeth; and to him that knocketh it shall be opened.

-St. Matthew 7:8

Tracy sat in the kitchen watching her mother frantically run around getting ready to leave for work. Tracy tried telling her about some of the problems she'd been having but her mother was just too distracted to hear a word of it.

"Mama, are you even listening?" Tracy asked after explaining her issues she'd been having with Jeremiah. There was no response.

"Ma!" Tracy asked again.

"Huh? What?" Her mother said whipping around to face her. Tracy just blankly stared.

"Oh, Tracy I'm sorry, I'm in a rush." Her mother said taking a quick breather, running her fingers through short brown hair. Suddenly her watch started to beep.

"Shoot! I'm going to be late." Her mother said quickly. She kissed Tracy's cheek, grabbed her bag and headed for the door.

"Tell Miah I love him," she said and left. Tracy rolled her eyes and got up from the kitchen table. Her mother always dreamed of teaching but never went to college. When her father was alive he paid for her mother to attend community college but since he's been gone her mother now worked three jobs to pay for it and the family finances. Tracy looked up at the clock, it was almost 7:30, and school starts at 8:00. She walked down the hall to Jeremiah's bedroom and knocked.

"Miah?" she called. There was no answer. "Jeremiah, we need to start getting ready to leave for school."

"Go away!" Tracy heard Jeremiah shout from behind the door.

"Miah can't we just talk about this?" Tracy said.

"No." He shouted again. Tracy sighed, signifying her defeat. She grabbed her backpack from off the living room couch and books off the kitchen counter and left out the front door. Tracy walked down the dirty, grungy stairs of the apartment building looking at her feet with every step she took. Her mind buzzed with problems; her father, her mother, Jeremiah and even herself. Tears began to drip from her eyes and she was oblivious to anyone around her until she was so distracted that she bumped into someone.

"Oh gosh!" Tracy said, helping the person up. "I'm sorry."

"It's no problem." He said.

"Are you ok?" Tracy asked.

"I'm fine," he said picking up Tracy's books that had scattered all over the sidewalk.

"Thanks," Tracy said as they handed her books.

"You're welcome, so what's your name?" He asked.

"I'm Tracy." Tracy said.

"I'm-uh…Jack." He said. Tracy and Jack shook hands. When they let go a random gust of air came through, just like before at the grave yard. Tracy shivered and zipped up her jacket. Jack looked up at the sky and smiled. Tracy then saw him wink and gasped.

"Um uh, I've got to get to school." Tracy said and quickly walked away.

"Oh, well, I'll see you around." Jack called.

"Hopefully not," Tracy said under her breath.

Chapter 6

**Evil pursueth sinner: but to the righteous
good shall be repayed.**

-Proverbs 13:21

Jeremiah slowly opened his bedroom door and poked his head out in the hallway. He smiled to himself when he saw that there was no sign of Tracy or his mom. His body was still buzzing from last night. His heart was racing at high speed. He grabbed his backpack and left the apartment. As he walked down the street he began to feel weak. His buzz started to wind down and his heart beat slowed down to its normal speed. As Jeremiah approached the school he felt as if he desperately needed sleep. He put his books away in his locker and went to class. By third period Jeremiah was beat. As he walked to fourth period he was pulled out of the schools back door.

"Hey, let go of me." Jeremiah shouted, kicking and punching, flinging his books everywhere.

"Miah, dog you need to chill out." A familiar voice cried. Jeremiah held still and saw Calvin, Theo and the rest of the gang. Calvin was tall, dark and dangerous. He looked like a thug, talked like a thug, walked like a thug, dressed like a thug, heck he was a thug. No one messed with him. Lucky for Jeremiah, they ran in the same pack. They were cool.

"Ay C." Jeremiah said as they tapped knuckles. "What's the deal? I have to get to class."

"Man, class is for suckers. I got somethin' way hot, you with it!?" Calvin said. He then dug in his jacket pocket and pulled out a plastic bag filled with white powder and cigarettes. "Besides I thought you could use another hit." He said waving the plastic bag in Jeremiah's face. Jeremiah didn't think twice. He grabbed the bag and stuffed it in his pants pocket.

"So where we going?" he asked.

"It's not where we're going it's what we're doing." Calvin said slyly.

"Huh?" Jeremiah asked again.

"Man, just come on." Theo said.

Chapter 7

**A friend loveth at all times, and a
brother is born for adversity.**

-Proverbs 17:17

Tracy sat in her Trigonometry class, intently looking at the clock. Her teacher Mr. Sullivan was uninteresting. He had to be at least eighty-years old; he had gray hair and wrinkled skin. He looked like Eurkle only a lot older. *Brrring!* The bell sounded. Tracy grabbed her stuff and like her peers, bolted out of the classroom. She went to her locker to put her books away. She grabbed her paper brown lunch bag and walked down the hall to the cafeteria. She found an empty table over in the corner of the room, so she sat down and began to eat her lunch.

"Hi Tracy," a voice said. Tracy looked up from her turkey sandwich and saw her old friends, Karri, Amber and Evie.

"Hi." Tracy replied, turning her attention back to her sandwich. Karri, Amber and Evie took a seat at the table. Karri had cream colored skin and shoulder length jet black hair. Amber had mocha colored skin and wore her long dark brown hair up in a swept back ponytail. Evie had a chocolate skin color and wore her dark brown hair in micro braids with honey blond streaks.

"How you been?" Evie asked. Tracy shrugged her shoulders.

"Good I guess." Tracy said solemnly.

"We haven't seen you around much." Amber said, "It's like you don't want to be our friend anymore." Tracy sat silently and fiddled with her juice box.

"Look Tracy we want to see if you're coming to the movies with us next Friday for my birthday. I'll be seventeen on Monday." Karri said, "You didn't forget, did you?"

"No, Karri I didn't forget." Tracy said as she felt tears swell up in her throat. "But I'm going to have to pass." Tracy got up from the table.

"Tracy," Evie said in a questioning tone, as Tracy packed up her lunch. Tracy looked at her.

"Why don't you like hanging out with us anymore?" Evie asked. "Since your dad died you've completely shut us out." Evie put her hand on Tracy shoulder. "If you need to talk "

"I'm sorry, I have to go." Tracy said, cutting Evie off in mid-sentence. She brushed away Evie's hand and left the cafeteria.

Chapter 8

Thou shall not steal.

-Exodus 20:15

"Stop thief," the store owner shouted. "Help! I'm being robbed." Jeremiah poked his head out from behind the alley wall. He saw Calvin, Theo and the rest of the gang running down the street from Mr. Al-Kuaji's General store. Mr. Al-Kuaji was short and plump. He was from Kuwait and had cigar tan skin color. He'd owned the general store for over twenty years. He sold everything and anything you'd ever need. His store was so packed with stuff it almost impossible to make a complete circle without bumping in to something.

"Rotten kids!" he shouted as he threw tomatoes, lettuce and even rocks at them.

"Run Miah," Theo shouted as he and the others ran past Jeremiah. Jeremiah took off behind them, with Mr. Al-Kuaji right on their tail, waving around a broom.

"Get back here." He screamed. Jeremiah and the others boys ran even faster.

"Split up." Calvin cried. Jeremiah cut left through the park, jumped the fence behind the basketball court and ran, home free.

Chapter 9

**For he shall give his angels charge over
thee, to keep thee in all thy ways.**

-Psalm 91:11

It was three o'clock and the bell signaling the end of the day had just rung. Tracy went to her locker and packed up her stuff. She walked out of the school building and began her three mile walk to the grocery store.

"You're late again, Tracy," said a short Chinese man, wearing a green smock with a gold badge that read "Manager" in black letters.

"I'm sorry Mr. Dong." Tracy quickly replied.

"No more apologies." Mr. Dong snapped and walked away in a huff. Tracy rolled her eyes. She went to the back, put up her stuff, put on her green smock and went to work.

"Tracy." Mr. Dong called. Tracy looked up from the cash register and over at Mr. Dong.

"Yes sir?" Tracy answered.

"Clean up on aisle three. Some kid knocked over the pyramid of tomatoes." Mr. Dong said.

"I'm kind of busy." Tracy said as she watched a white young woman, with bright blond hair, begin to unload her shopping cart. "Can't you get someone else?" But Mr. Dong was already out of earshot. Tracy rolled her eyes again and took a deep sigh.

"Ay, Tracy," a voice said. Tracy turned to see Brian. He was light skin, had straight dark brown hair and big brown puppy dog eyes. Brian was mixed, not the typical Black and White boy. He was Latina and Black. He and Tracy were members of the same church. They had known each other for some time and grew even closer after Tracy started working at the store.

"Hey Brian," Tracy said ringing the young woman up.

"I didn't see you at church on Sunday." Brian said.

"Do you ever?" Tracy said sarcastically. Brian grimaced at her outburst.

"I'm sorry Brian." Tracy said.

"Mr. Dong giving you a hard time?" Brian asked.

"This time he wants me to clean up the pyramid of tomatoes."

"I'll finish this up for you while you clean it up if you want." Brian said pointing at the cash register.

"But isn't your shift over?" Tracy asked eyeing the backpack on his shoulder. He shrugged. "Thanks Brian." Tracy grabbed the mop and bucket from the custodian closet and went down aisle three to clean up the mess.

"I'll keep you in my prayers Tracy." Brian called to her.

"Hi Tracy," a familiar voice said. Tracy quickly spun around.

"What are you doing here...uh?"

"Jack." Jack said as a puzzled look crossed Tracy's face. "I was in the neighborhood."

"So you came here? A grocery store?" she asked. Jack shrugged his shoulders.

"I just follow orders." He said.

"Jack, you're starting to creep me out." Tracy said wearily, as she continued to clean up the tomatoes.

"I don't mean to." Jack said. "I'm trying to do my job."

"What job?" Tracy asked as she turned around to face him but he was gone…like he disappeared in thin air.

Chapter 10

And I say also unto thee, That thou art Peter, and upon this rock I will build my church; and the gates of hell shall not prevail against it.

-St. Matthew 16:18

Jeremiah watched as the sun set behind the buildings in the distance. He wondered down the street on his way back to the alley to meet back up with the others. A random gust of wind came through, sending a shiver down Jeremiah's spine. He brushed it off and kept walking. He looked up ahead as he heard someone walking towards him. It was an older woman. She had dark, wrinkled skin. Her black, gray streaked hair was pulled back into a bun with a purple feathered hat on top and she was dressed in a purple suit. Jeremiah watched as she crossed the street towards the church. He stopped and stared up at the colorful stain glass windows of the building. Jeremiah quickly crossed the street after he saw that woman had gone into the church. He gazed up at the wooden cross on the roof.

He seemed mesmerized. It was early Sunday morning. The sun had just peeked up through the horizon. Like every Sunday morning

Jeremiah and his family got up and went to church. "Jeremiah" his father called, "come put on your shoes." Jeremiah stood in his bedroom mirror checking his tie. He yawned and scratched his head.

"I'm coming, pops." Jeremiah said. Jeremiah turned off his light and walked down the hall into the living room.

"Miah, hurry up." His mother nagged, "I don't want to be late."

"Ebony, calm down," his father said. "He's moving as fast as he can."

"Mama, I can't find my bible." Tracy complained, storming into the room.

"It's on the kitchen counter where you left it, T." Her mother said, "Miah, are you ready yet?"

"Yes mama." Jeremiah answered, as he slipped on his dress shoes. "I'm ready.

"Tracy!" Her father called, "let's go."

"I'm coming daddy." Tracy said.

"Baby, fix your tie." Her mother told her father.

"I'll do it on the way." He said. "T!"

"I'm here." Tracy said walking into the room. Jeremiah grabbed his bible from off the coffee table and followed his family out the door.

"What a mighty God we serve…" his father began to sing as he closed the front door, "What a mighty God we serve…"

"Excuse me," a voice said. Jeremiah flinched, a little surprised.

"Excuse me son," the voice said again. Jeremiah looked over at the doors of the church. A man with a caramel skin tone, big round hazel eyes and a clean shaven head stood dressed in a suit. Next to him stood a woman with a mocha skin tone and long spiral curled hair.

"They must be tracks," Jeremiah thought as glanced at the woman's hair, "so fake." Holding the woman's hand was a little girl with braids. She appeared to be about seven years old. She had a mocha skin tone, just like the woman, big round hazel eyes, just like the man, and she was dressed in a puffy pink dress with black dress shoes and white stockings. Her braids were tied out of her face with a pink ribbon. She held a bible in her other hand.

"Are you coming in?" The man asked. Jeremiah froze up. Another random gust of wind came through. He took a step forward, nodding his head. All of a sudden he stopped, looked up at the cross, backed away and he quickly crossed the street and ran.

Chapter 11

Likewise, I say unto you, there is joy in the presence of the angels of God over one sinner that repenteth.

-St. Luke 15:10

Tracy sat Indian style on the living room couch. She stared out the window, hoping to see her younger brother on his way home. It was ten fifty-seven; the street lights had come almost four hours ago. Jeremiah had been late before but not like this. Tracy lay back, thinking of all the horrible this that could happen to a thirteen-year-old boy alone on the streets at this time of night. She stared up at the ceiling and thought of Jack, of how strange he seemed to her. Then she rolled over and fell asleep.

Hours later Tracy awoke at a sound of the door knob turning. She quickly sat up as she watched a figure stumble and wobble through the doorway in the dark. It was Jeremiah. He walked, almost fumbled down the hall, dropping something on his way to his bedroom and shut the door behind him. Tracy got up and flicked on the light. She looked over at the middle of the hallway and saw a plastic bag. Tracy picked it up and examined it. The bag was filled with white powder and cigarettes.

"No." Tracy thought to herself. "Miah would never." Tracy opened the bag and sniffed the powder. She stormed down the hall and pushed Miah's bedroom door open.

"Cocaine," Tracy screamed in anger, flicking on the lights. Jeremiah jumped up out of bed and glared at his sister.

"What's got you hot, T!?" Jeremiah asked rubbing his eye.

"Have you been doing this stuff!" she shouted shoving the plastic bag in his face. Miah's eyes widened, he quickly jumped up and started searching his room.

"You're not going to find it Miah," Tracy screamed, "it's here in my hand."

"Shut up, T!" Jeremiah whispered firmly trying to snatch the bag out of Tracy's hand, "you're going to wake up mama."

"What is this?" Tracy snapped, waving the bag around. "Have you been-?"

"It's nothing." Jeremiah snapped back, cutting Tracy off and snatching the bag away. Tracy stood there shocked as she watched him put the bag away under his pillow.

"It's nothing." Tracy said grabbing his arm. She gazed into his eyes. They were bloodshot red. "Miah, how could you?"

"It's easy, T! Just take the cigarette, scrape out the tobacco crap and slip in the good stuff." Jeremiah wheezed.

"Why do you care, T?" He mumbled pulling away. "It's not like I'm hurting anybody."

"If mama knew what you were doing it would kill her and you know it." Tracy said.

"Mama…" He whipped around. "She can't ever get wind of this."

"She's going to." Tracy said.

"I promise to God, T if you tell mama I'll…" Jeremiah screamed.

"You'll do what?!" Tracy shouted back. Jeremiah just glared at her, his eyes burning with hatred toward his sister. Sweat dripped from his forehead as he raised his fist in the air, ready to strike. Suddenly a random gust of air filled the room. He felt nauseous and room began to spin. He stopped and wiped the sweat from his face.

"Just get out of my room." He said as he slid to the floor.

Chapter 12

Jesus therefore, knowing all things that should come upon him, went forth, and said unto them, *whom seek ye?*

-St. John 18:4

It was 4:00 A.M. as Jeremiah lay in his bed and stared at his ceiling. He sat soaking in hatred. His body ached, his head raced, pounding like a drum and he felt emotionally and physically drained. He had to do something, he had to get away. He desperately needed rest, no, he needed another hit. Jeremiah got up and threw on some clothes. He walked down the hallway to the front door and snuck out. When he got outside he took a deep breath, letting the cool, refreshing morning air fill his lungs. He started up the street, heading for the gangs spot. He stopped suddenly as he heard something; footsteps. Jeremiah turned around and saw a figure, a dark figure, walking toward him. His body tense, his brow began to sweat, his jaw tightened and he stood very still, almost life less. The figure came closer and closer. Jeremiah finally saw that it was a boy who looked to be about Tracy's age. The boy walked up to him and stopped

"What's a kid like you doing out so early in the morning?" The boy asked.

"What's it to you?" Jeremiah replied.

"Chill out, man" The boy laughed. Jeremiah just rolled his eyes and started to walk off.

"But really, where are you going?" The boy asked following Jeremiah.

"You wouldn't be one you're way to get another hit, would you?" Jeremiah though back to the argument he'd had with Tracy before he left. He suddenly felt overwhelmed with hatred, guilt and greed. He turned away.

"I'm Jack, by the way." The boy added.

"I'm Jeremiah." Jeremiah mumbled, still not looking.

"I know who you are." Jack said. Jeremiah turned to face him but Jack was gone.

Chapter 13

**My help cometh from the LORD,
which made heaven and earth**

-Psalm 121:2

Tracy arrived at her apartment building after ending a long day at school followed by an even more stressful day at work. She was beat. Tracy thought about the day she'd had, especially Amber, Evie and Karri who came over to talk to her during lunch period for the third day in a row.

"Tracy, please talk to us." Evie begged.

"There's nothing to talk about." Tracy mumbled.

"We all know something's wrong, T," Amber said. "We're worried about you. Is it your dad; your mother? Who is it Miah?" Tracy shrugged in frustration. She wished they'd just leave her alone.

"We just want to help, T. That's all." Karri whispered wrapping her arm Tracy. Tracy pulled away.

"Thank you but I just need my space." She replied getting up and walked away.

Tracy walked up the steps to her floor as her thoughts flickered to Jack.

"Tracy!" Jack had called out to her. Tracy had turned around to see him pushing himself through the crowd of students. She walked faster and swerved her way through. She looked over her shoulder and saw that she'd lost him. She slowed down her pace, still looking over her shoulder.

"Tracy." A voice chirped. Tracy turned her head around to find Jack standing right in front of her. She did a double take.

"How did you? Why did you?" Tracy stuttered. Jack just smiled.

"What do you want?!" Tracy asked. Jack's expression turned serious. A random gust of wind came through, it howled. Jack looked up and breathed it in. "I'll tell her." Jack mumbled, looking at the sky. Tracy's heart rate sped up as he turned his attention back to her.

"It's Jeremiah." He said.

"My brother? Wait, how do you..."

"I can't say, Tracy." He responded, cutting her off.

"Is he hurt?" Tracy blurted out, grabbing Jack shoulder. He shook his head.

"No. He's safe but-" He began.

"Why am I listening to you?" Tracy asked herself aloud. "I don't even know you."

"I know you." Jack whispered.

"No, you don't." She said and began walking away.

"Tracy, be careful. Jeremiah, he's not himself!" He watched her walk away. He looked to the sky one last time and shrugged his shoulders

Tracy pulled out her key when she arrived at her door but before she even put her key in the lock the door flew open.

"Mama?" Tracy gasped, a little puzzled, as she saw her mother standing in the doorway.

"Tracy, it's just you." Her mother said stepping aside to let Tracy in.

"Sorry to disappoint you." Tracy replied as she tossed her backpack to the couch.

"Oh, T you know I didn't mean it like that."

"Mama, why are you home? You didn't lose your job did you?"

"No, nothing like that, I took the day off." She took a deep breath and pulled a plastic bag out of her back pocket. "I found this on the floor next to Miah's bed." It was the bag of drugs. The same bag Tracy had found Jeremiah with a few days ago.

"Tracy, has he been doing this stuff?" Tracy looked away, unable to look into her mother's fearful eyes.

"Tracy?"

"Yes ma'am."

"So you knew about this?" Her mother asked. Tracy nodded.

"When were you going to tell me?"

"When were you going to have time to listen?" Tracy snapped

"Tracy…" Her mother paused and began to cry.

"Oh no, mama please don't cry." Tracy pleaded as she began to tear up herself.

"I'm sorry, T. This is my fault. I haven't been a good mother. I should have known."

"No, mama, I'm sorry. I should have done a better job at taking charge while you were at work."

"It's just that since…your dad died, I've been taking all those extra jobs to make up for his lost salary."

"Are things really that bad mama?" Tracy said. Her mother grabbed her hand and nodded as more tears ran down her face.

"Yeah, baby, it is." She nodded. Tracy shook her head and thought.

"Mama, I've been praying. Help's got to be on its way." Her mother wiped her eyes and shrugged.

"I just don't know what to do, T." She said.

"You're going through college." Tracy replied, "You'll find-"

"No, I won't. I've looked everywhere; no school in the area needs a teacher." Her mother said cutting her off. "I'm sunk."

Chapter 14

But they that wait upon the Lord shall renew their strength…they shall run, and not be weary…

-Isaiah 40:31

Hours had passed. The sky was gray and the street lights were on, Tracy lay peacefully asleep on the couch. She began to stir, tossing & turning and mumbling to herself. Tracy's eyes suddenly flashed wide open. She sat up and wiped the cold sweat from her forehead. She quickly got up, grabbed her jacket and sprinted out the front door.

"What am I doing?" Tracy thought to herself as she zipped down the stairs. "The dream, the alley, Jeremiah, danger," Tracy thought to herself. Then Tracy came to a halt, as Jack came to her mind.

"Tracy, be careful. Jeremiah, he's not himself!" She'd remembered he had said. The air was frigid. It bit her ears, stung her lips and burned her fingers. She took a deep breath letting the cool air intertwine with her thoughts as a random gust of air came through. She shook it off and started back down the block in a sprint.

Chapter 15

But I say unto you. That whosoever is angry with his brother without a cause shall be in danger of the judgment: and whosoever shall say to his brother, Raca, shall be in danger of the council: but whosoever shall say, Thou fool, shall be in danger of hell fire.

-St. Matthew 5: 22

Jeremiah stood in the alley, laughing and joking around with the rest of the gang. It was late. The sky black and the street lights were dim. The city seemed a buzz, no wait, it was just him. He took a swig of the liquor that was being passed around. It burned his throat; he almost choked but forced himself to hold it down.

"Way to go Miah," Theo joked. Jeremiah smiled as he put a cigarette to his lips, taking a hit.

"Ay, Miah why are you smoking that soft stuff?" Denny chuckled. The others bust out laughing. Jeremiah didn't see what was so funny but laughed none the less. It's crazy what that stuff does to you.

"Come hit some more of this." Denny said taking another hit of his cocaine and handing it over to Jeremiah. He shook his head and turned Denny's hand away.

"Nah, it's ok. I'm trying to go light tonight." Jeremiah said shoving his hands into his pocket.

"Listen to him, 'I'm trying to go light tonight.'" A boy name Shaun mimicked. Jeremiah glared at Shaun's dilated pupils and wished he could leave a black mark around his light-skinned eye as everyone laughed. Jeremiah sucked his teeth, grabbed the cocaine and took a long, hard hit. A few more hits and a couple swigs of liquor, Jeremiah was higher than anyone in the alley. Jeremiah lay in a pile of garbage bags and started to nod off until Calvin began to speak.

"I never thought you could do it, Miah." He said.

"Wazzzhat, C?" Jeremiah smiled looking over at him.

"Be one of us." He said walking over to him. Jeremiah just sat there smiling, not knowing what to say.

"Look, you've come a long way but before I official accept your membership in the crew, there's some business I want to take care off." Calvin said slyly.

"What'd ya have in mind?" Jeremiah laughed.

"Jeremiah?!" a voice cried. Jeremiah turned to see Tracy. He smiled and ran up to his older sister.

"T!" He cried and kissed her sloppily on the cheek. Tracy wiped off the spit and looked around in disgust.

"Miah, what are you doing?" Tracy asked.

"Jus' hangin' out," he said hanging all over her. Tracy held her nose, trying hard not to smell anymore of Jeremiah's horrible breath. It smelled rancid, like vodka and a burning coco tree.

"What are you on?" Tracy shouted.

"Traacy you got to try this ssstuff." Jeremiah said slurring his words. The boys laughed at him as he grabbed a bottle of vodka and chugged it down. Tracy shook her head as she held back tears. She grabbed the bottle and threw it at the brick wall. It shattered all over the ground.

"Come on, we're going home." Tracy said pulling her brother by the arm.

"Aw, isn't that cute. Miah's big sister's here to carry him home." Theo snickered.

"Miah, man are you going to let her control you like that." Shaun said. "She has you on a short leash." Jeremiah shook his head as anger and hatred instantly began to come over him. He ripped away from Tracy's grip.

"No, Tracy. I'm not cool with that."

"Miah, don't be ridiculous." Tracy shouted back. "You're coming home." She reached for him. He backed away. She reached for him again and he pushed her. Tracy looked stunned.

"Get lost. I'm not leavin'."

"What?" Tracy gasped.

"He said he's not leavin'." Calvin repeated. "Tell her Miah."

"Tracy, I hate you. Why God ever gave me loser for a sister like you, I'll never know." Miah snapped. "You know what, I hate God too!" Tracy stood speechless as hot tears began to fall.

"Miah," She stuttered. She couldn't breathe and gasped for air.

"Don't cry! You cry over everything, just shut up." She continued to cry, who was this boy, where was her brother? Jeremiah's heart rate speed up and his head raced. He felt so angry, so furious, so sad, so scared, so…evil.

"I said shut the crying up, Tracy!" He screamed. His hands clenched into a fist. He threw his fist up and hit Tracy's face like a bullet. Tracy screamed in pain and held her nose and mouth. The others cheered and applauded. Jeremiah stood catching his breath, he felt weak as if he too might cry. Tracy's nose and mouth was covered in blood. Jeremiah noticed a figure at the entry way of the alley. It was Jack, the boy he'd met not too long ago.

"Get out of here Tracy." Jeremiah shouted. Tracy ran without another word, not even noticing Jack. Jeremiah turned his attention back to the mysterious boy. Jack stood and stared all around, eyeing him at the same time.

"The blood of Jesus is against you." He said simply and ran after Tracy. Jeremiah felt a chill run through his body. He shivered as a random gust of air came through.

"What did I just do?" He thought. Calvin walked up to Jeremiah and smiled.

"Now, about that business," he said.

Chapter 16

And when the woman saw that she was not hid, she came trembling, and falling down before him, she declared unto him before all the people for what cause she had touched him, and how she was healed immediately. And he said unto her, *Daughter, be of good comfort: thy faith hath made thee whole; go in peace.*

-St. Luke 8:47-48

Tracy ran. She didn't look back, only ahead, straight ahead. Her eyes squinted as the sun peaked over the horizon. She didn't know where her feet were taking her but there was no way of stopping them.

"Tracy." a voice called. Tracy ignored it.

"Tracy!" called voice called again. A random gust of air came through; Tracy started to slow down and then came to a sudden stop, taking in the air. She dropped to her knees and let out a cry. Tears started to run down her cheeks again.

"Tracy," the voice whispered. Tracy turned to the voice as she felt a firm hand on her shoulder. It was Jack. She looked up at him and stared into his eyes. He looked away and up at the star lit sky.

"God will make a way, Tracy."

"Miah hit me, Jack."

"He's always going to be there for you." Jack said, ignoring Tracy's soft voice.

"Jack, did you hear me? He hit me. Miah hit me." Tracy shouted, jumping to her feet, feeling the same anger over take her that took over Jeremiah.

"Tracy, God-"

"I curse His name." Tracy screamed and turned away.

"You don't mean that," Jack whispered. "Neither did Jeremiah." Tracy wiped her face and shook his head.

"Don't let the devil control you." He said firmly, "Don't give him the satisfaction of taking over another one of God's children. The devil is a liar."

"I'm done with you, with both of you." Tracy said and turned to walk away. Jack grabbed her arm and swung her around.

"Look where God has brought you."

"Where?" Tracy snapped. "Jack, look at my face." Tracy wiped her nose and mouth and stuck her hand in his face, eager to show him fresh blood. She looked at her hand, it was clean. There was nothing; not a thing. The blood was gone. Her hands, her face, her shirt, were clean. Tracy stopped and thought for a moment. The pain was gone too.

"Look where God has brought you." Jack cried again. Tracy looked up. She saw stain glass windows and a big wooden cross. "He died for our sins and rose again. He is our protector, our provider. He will make a way." Tracy walked up to the cross and kneeled on her knees, tears of joy flowed from her eyes.

"Call on His name." Jack said.

"Jesus." She whispered, tasting the sweet sensation.

Chapter 17

**Let everything that hath breath praise
the Lord. Praise ye the Lord.**

-Psalm 150:6

Tracy stood at the doors of the church, pacing back and forth, while Jack stood watching her. Tracy hadn't seen Jeremiah since the night at the alley, she was worried and scared but something else had taken Jeremiah's place for the moment. Jack had talked Tracy into going back to church with him. She has been excited about it all morning until she reached the church doors. Tracy stopped pacing and wiped the sweat from her forehead.

"Tracy, what's the problem?" Jack asked.

"Jack, I don't know if I can do this."

"Why not?"

"I haven't been here in so long, what will Pastor Lawrence say? What will my friends, what will everyone think?"

"Look Tracy, I can't make you do anything. I especially can't make you go to church for me or anyone else. You have to go for you."

Tracy stopped and closed her eyes.

"Lord, give me strength." She whispered to herself. She took a deep breath, a random gust of air came through, and it closed up around her and slowly died down as she exhaled. Tracy pushed the church doors open and was overwhelmed with happiness. Music from the band blared so loudly that she could feel the vibrations running through her entire body. The choir voices blew her away.

"Hold on my brother don't give up, hold on my sister just look up..." The choir sang. "There is a master plan in store for you if you just make it through..."

Tracy smiled and fought back tears that began to collect in her throat. She looked around and spotted Evie, Amber and Karri. Tracy let go of her fears and slid in the pew next to them. Karri was the first to notice. She nudged Evie who nudged Amber. They turned their attention from the choir to Tracy who stood clapping to the beat. They said nothing to each other and nothing to Tracy, they didn't have to. Memories of past Sundays jumped out of Tracy's mind as she looked around at her church family. She thought and remember; Her father getting so moved by the spirit he'd cry out to the Lord every minute, her mother fanning herself and every once in a while raising her hand whispering "Preach it, pastor!" or "Yes, Lord, yes." Refraining herself from having to nudge Jeremiah hard in the side to keep him from falling asleep on her shoulder.

"Today is the first day of the best days of your life...the best...the best is yet to come!" The choir sang...and sang...and sang.

Chapter 18

I press toward the mark for the prize of the high calling of God in Christ Jesus.

-Philippians 3:14

The church doors swung open and out walked Tracy, Amber, Evie, Karri and Brian. Morning service had just ended and everyone was either headed home or hanging around the church just talking about Pastor's powerful message. Tracy fought back tears as she walked down the street with her friends. They weren't tears of sadness; or were they? She didn't know, her stomach crumpled and her head raced with thoughts about Pastor's message, God, Jeremiah, her mother, her father and friends. One thing seemed to lead to another.

"Glory Hallelujah!" Brian cried out, "For He is good and worthy to be praised."

"That was a good service, huh." Karri stated.

"It sure was girlfriend." Amber said.

"I love how the choir got down this morning." Evie laughed. Amber looked over at Tracy who was in a daze, just staring straight ahead. Karri soon noticed and smiled at Brian. Brain stopped and jumped in front of Tracy, startling her and scaring her out of her daze.

"Brian!" Tracy gasped. Brian looked at Tracy and Tracy looked at him.

"I've been praying for you, Tracy." Brian said resting his hand on her shoulder.

"I know, Brian." Tracy said as a smile spread across her lips. "Thanks."

"I'm really happy that you decided to come back to church. It shows that God is a way maker." Brian said. "Tracy, no matter how hard things may seem always remember that God is a way maker and that the reason things are so hard are so he can reveal himself and show that you've got to make a change."

"God's got a plan, Tracy." Evie jumped in. "Not your will, but His will." Tracy smiled and was filled with an overwhelming feeling of warmth. At that moment a random gust of air came through, Tracy said goodbye to her friends and walked home. Something troubled her, a question she kept asking herself over and over as she arrived at her building; "Where in the world was Jack?"

Chapter 19

**For the Lord knoweth the way of the righteous:
but the way of the ungodly shall perish.**

-Psalm 1:6

Jeremiah's prison cell was dirty. It was cold too. He sat in the corner, curled up trying to keep warm, also to keep himself and the cockroaches that were crawling all over the cement floor as far from each other as possible. Jeremiah was alone and scared. He was angry too. He was in trouble.

"Ain't too much fun is it?" a voice said. Jeremiah look up, on the other side of the bars stood Jack. Jeremiah didn't say anything as Jack's last words played in his head; "The blood of Jesus is against you."

"What's up, Miah?" Jack asked.

"Don't you see where I'm at? You know what's up." Jeremiah said sarcastically.

"Miah, you know what you did was wrong." Jack said breaking the bone chilling silence.

"Police chief told you, huh?"

"The Chief," Jack nodded, "right." Jeremiah placed his face in his hands and sighed deeply.

"But before all this, that night, when Tracy showed up at the alley, I was so high. I didn't know what I was doing. After you took off after Tracy, Calvin took advantage of my anger. He knew I wanted in the crew and dangled the membership in my face every chance he got. He was finally going to let me in but I had to do one thing for him first. I didn't want to but I really wanted in to the crew." Jeremiah said.

"So you robbed Mr. Al-Kuaji?" Jack asked. Jeremiah shrugged his shoulders.

"I tried," he replied. "There was this new liquor Mr. Al-Kuaji had just got in stock. Calvin said it was some strong stuff, he said it would give you a different feeling than anything you've had before. Stronger than beer, hits harder than cocaine and more addictive than marijuana, C wanted it bad."

"I want it." Calvin said.

"But how are you going to get it?" Jeremiah asked.

"You," Calvin replied like He had just been asked a question to which the answer was obvious.

"Say what?"

"Miah, man, don't be a punk." Theo snapped. Jeremiah sucked his teeth.

"I'm not being a punk. I'm just not slick like you guys."

"Don't give me that." Calvin snapped. "Go back to your sister with that sissy stuff."

"That's not funny, man."

"Wasn't supposed to be," Calvin snarled, getting up in Jeremiah's face. Shaun put a firm hand on Calvin's shoulder, pulling him back.

"What if I get caught?" Jeremiah asked after Calvin's facial expression had changed.

"You're not goin' to get caught?" Calvin said, "we have you're back."

"C, nah." Jeremiah said, shaking his head. "I'm just not cool with this."

"Look Miah, you do this and you're officially a member of the crew. You chose." Calvin said.

"This is it, right?"

"Yeah, man." Calvin said with a sly grin.

"What happened then?" Jack asked. Jeremiah looked up at Jackson and took a deep breath.

"I got caught." He said. "I was so nervous. I was sure everyone in the store knew what was running through my mind and Mr. Al-Kuaji was eyeing me good. I walked over to the fridge and stared at the bottles for a minute, I acted like was getting a Mountain Dew. When I thought I was clear I grabbed the liquor bottle, slipped it into my jacket and walked out. I saw the crew waiting at the corner. I took my time walking over to them, suddenly they took off runnin'. I turned around and saw Mr. Al-Kuaji coming toward me with a broom. I ran too. Mr. Al-Kuaji swatted me with the broom and I tripped and fell, the bottle slipped from my jacket and shattered on the sidewalk. He grabbed me and twisted my arms behind my back so I wouldn't get away. The crew was still running ahead. 'Guys, help me!' 'Calvin, Theo!' I called out but they just kept running and left me there. Mr. Al-Kuaji dragged me back to his store and called the cops. Now here I am." Jack didn't say anything for a while and neither did Jeremiah.

"What are you thinking now?" Jack finally asked.

"I'm thinking I don't want to go to Juvie. I need to apologize to Tracy and quit the crew. I'm thinking I just want to go home." Miah said. "The blood of Jesus is against me."

"Not you Miah, the devil." Jack said.

"For God so loved the world that He gave His only begotten Son, that whoever believeth in him should not perish but have everlasting life." Jeremiah stated. "I wonder how much God loves the world now. I wonder if he loves me, even I cursed his name."

"God commended His love toward us, in that, while we were yet sinner, Christ died for us." Jack said with a smile.

"Huh?" Miah asked.

"Jeremiah, God loves you no matter what you do. No matter how stupid. He's already forgiven you. That's what makes Him so great, His love, His grace and His mercy. He hasn't forgotten you." Jack said.

"Then why am I here?" Miah snapped.

"Look, when things get bad, you don't ask why me, you ask God what it is He wants you to do." Jack said calmly.

"Again, huh?"

"How else was God supposed to get you away from those boys? You wouldn't answer His other calls. He had to get your attention."

"His other calls?" Miah said in disbelief.

"Tracy's been warning you about those boys, Miah." Jack said, "But you just wouldn't hear it. And when you got chased by Mr. Al-Kuaji the first time, you knew what the others did. You know the only thing that's been keeping you alive from all those drugs the Lord. You got off easy, you could be dead right now but God spared you and let you see another day." Jeremiah wiped his face before Jack could see the tears that began to form in his eyes.

"Think about it." Jack whispered. Suddenly a random gust of air came through. Jeremiah didn't shiver; he let it come upon him. It howled slightly, like a whisper in his ear, "Miah". He closed his eyes and listened.

"Jesus." He whispered.

"Miah."

"Jesus,"

"Miah."

"Jesus." He called.

"Miah!" Jeremiah opened his eyes and on the other side of the bars, stood Tracy. He quickly wiped his eyes and stood up. He walked over to the bars.

"Tracy." He stuttered.

"Darn it Miah, what've you done now?"

"How'd you know I was here?"

"Mama left a note on the fridge telling me what happened, to come see you. Is she here?"

"You missed her by an hour. She had to get to work." Jeremiah said, stepped back from the bars and turned away from his sister.

"Tracy," he whispered after a long period of silence. "I'm sorry; so very sorry."

"Miah, it's ok."

"No T," he said shaking his head. "It's not. Mama and Pops raised me better than that, better than this." Tracy sighed.

"And you've been too good of a sister to me." He added. "I'm sorry for everything. All the problems I caused."

"Forgive and don't forget." Tracy replied. "No skin off my bones." Tracy reached her hands through the iron bars and Jeremiah grabbed them, squeezing them tight.

"I love you." He said, as a tear rolled down his cheek.

"I love you too." Tracy smiled, wiping away his tear. The devil is a liar.

Chapter 20

**Submit yourselves therefore to God. Resist
the devil, and he will flee from you.**

-James 4:7

Tracy sat anxiously on the couch, waiting for her mother to return
from court with Jeremiah. The front door swung open and Tracy shot
up as she saw her family stroll in.

Jeremiah's eyes wandered around the room and settled on his
older sister's gaze. He slowly made his way over to her and embraced
her. It'd been exactly three weeks and four days since she had last seen
him, he was held in custody until his court date. Tracy fought back
tears, her brother was home again.

"I really missed you, T."

"I missed you too, Miah."

"Mama, what did the judge say," she asked, as their mother sat
down at the kitchen table.

"Jeremiah has to complete three-hundred hours of community
service and has to attend classes at the YMCA for troubled kids for a

month." Their mother said, kicking off her heels. "It could have been less if he had turned in the names of those other boys."

"Ma, please don't." Jeremiah retorted calmly. She shook her head.

"I'm going to go get ready for work." She stretched her arms upward and yawned on her way to her bedroom. The door clicked shut and silence followed.

"I couldn't do it, ok." Jeremiah said out of the blue. Tracy turned to him. "I couldn't turn them in. I didn't want to."

"But why?"

"I learned some things sitting in that cell, T. Jack came and visited me a couple of times while I was there, you know. He'd come and talk to me about God and how everything would be alright if I'd trust in Him, and I did. I realized that I was sitting in there because God had singled me out from the rest of the crew for a reason. He was calling me and used the situation to get to me. It's crazy how He works, mysterious even but it shows how much He cares. Besides, maybe if they knew more about God they'd change their ways."

"You're a different person now, huh?"

"Yes and no; I'm still Miah but I don't belong to the streets anymore, I'm turning it over to God." He took a deep breath and got up. "I'm going to go pray, then straight to bed for me."

"Good night, Miah."

"Night, T."

Chapter 21

A double minded man is unstable in all his ways.

-James 1:8

The apartment was quiet and Jeremiah's bedroom was pitched black. He stared up at the ceiling, unable to rest. The sound of police sirens and dog's barking seeped through the walls. He threw back his covers and got up. He peeked out the window blinds and saw the city street below him; a homeless man pushing a shopping cart full earthly possessions, a drunk woman fumbling down the street and a couple of big guys hanging around a street light smoking cigarettes. He pulled on a pair of jeans, opened his bedroom door with a screech and tiptoed down the hallway. Jeremiah walked into the kitchen and looked up at the clock over the sink. 1:03 A.M. yeah they'd be out, he thought. He slipped on his shoes and slid out the front door. When he reached the first floor, he walked out the double doors, the cold air slapped him, he wished he was back in his bed fast asleep, but there was no turning back.

"Lord, give me strength." He whispered to himself as he walked past the big guys.

Tracy shot up from her slumber. She wiped away the sweat that dripped on her nose. She felt her cheeks, they were cold. She'd just had the strangest dream; a dark alley overwhelmed with the stench of alcohol and smoke, dark shadows and figures, a yell, a gunshot and then a bright warming light. "No," Tracy thought and then realized,

"Miah," she whispered aloud.

"Miah," she whispered again, throwing off the covers.

"Miah," she walked out into the hallway.

"Miah?" she knocked on his door. She walked in when there was no answer. "Miah?!"

"Oh, Miah," she says as she realized that her brother is long gone.

Chapter 22

**What time I am afraid, I will trust in thee. In God
I will praise his word, in God I have put my trust;
I will not fear what flesh can do unto me.**

-Psalm 56: 3-4

Jeremiah walked down the street, shivering with his hands in his jeans pockets. He spotted the alley, only steps ahead. He kept on walking. He had to do this; it was the only way out. Jeremiah stops at the edge of the alley entrance way. He takes a deep breath before stepping into the fog of grayish white smoke. He smells alcohol instantly and the odor of burning cocaine began to sink in to his skin. He felt dirty. He looked around and saw some of boys looking at him, conversing. Shaun turned around, stared but then smiled.

"Eh, it's Miah." He whispered.

"C, Miah's back." He said a little louder. Jeremiah stood still and held his ground, as he saw Calvin turn around and smile big. Theo walked up to him and laid a firm hand on his shoulder.

"Man, we thought you were a goner. Mr. Al-Kuaji don't play." He said. "Here, have it. You deserve it." He said, offering Jeremiah the beer bottle in his hand. Jeremiah shook his head and waved it away with his hand. He caught a glimpse of Denny passed out in the pile of garbage bags; nothing's changed here. Calvin walked up to him and led him deeper into the alley by the neck.

"I'm impressed, Miah, really I am."

"Why? I didn't get the drink."

"But it's the fact that you were willing to do it." Calvin said, "Anyone willing to do whatever it takes for the crew is our kind of guy. You're finally in."

"Besides, you can always try again." Calvin said, lighting a blunt. Jeremiah flinched.

"No."

"You say something?" Calvin asked, taking a hit.

"I said no." Jeremiah repeated, a little louder. Calvin looked puzzled.

"I'm done with this, with the alcohol, the drugs, the stealing, everything. I want out."

"That's real funny, Miah." Shaun joked.

"He didn't mean that C." Theo said. Calvin just stood and stared at Jeremiah, still smoking his weed.

"I mean it C. I want out."

"Miah," a voice said. Jeremiah turned to it and saw Tracy with fear in her eyes.

"T, what are you doing here?" He asked.

"Me? What are you doing here?" She replied. "I thought you changed." Jeremiah opened his mouth to reply but stopped when he heard a clicking sound. He turned back to Calvin, who now had a gun pointed right at him. Jeremiah's heart pumped faster. Tracy froze.

"Look, there's only one way out of this crew and it's not down the yellow brick road." Calvin said, lifting the gun up higher. "See you in Hell." A random gust of air, the shot fired, Tracy screamed, dogs barked, apartment lights flickered on, police sirens, the crew's fleeing footsteps, Tracy sobs, Jeremiah's wheezing and Jack's body lay still on the ground.

Chapter 23

Greater man hath no man than this, that a man lay down his life for his friends.

-St. John 15:13

Jack lay in the hospital bed while two doctors, dressed in white lab coats stood at the door conversing frantically. Tracy stood next to Jack's bed and held his hand, asking his over and over again where the pain was. He refused to tell her.

"Son, I'm a little shaken up right now, because, well, we can't find the bullet that hit you." One of the doctors said, walking up to Jack. "We see the bullet hole in your chest but you say you have very little pain. That's just down right strange."

"Doc, I'm fine." Jack said, sitting up.

"You sure are lucky." The doctor said.

"Luck had nothing to do with it." Jack replied. "I'm blessed."

"We're going to keep you here for a few days just to be safe and to run some more tests." The doctor said, now jotting down words on his clip board.

"I can't really do that Doc. I mean, I'm leaving tonight." Jack explained.

"Vacation or something?" the doctor asked.

"You could say that." Jack nodded.

"Well you'll just have to put it on hold." He said.

"That's not really up to me." Jack answered.

"You're staying and that's the end of it." The doctor said, walking out. Jack shook his head and chuckled a little.

"You find this amusing?" Tracy asked, sternly. Jack looked at her.

"You took a bullet for heaven sakes!" Tracy snapped, "And they can't even find it. Why aren't you more worried?"

"I have nothing to worry about."

"Shouldn't you call your parents and tell them?"

"My parents, they passed on years ago." Jack stated.

"Oh." Tracy said embarrassed. "I'm sorry. I forget I'm not the only one with a dead parent."

"My parents are still very much alive." Tracy looked up at him.

"Jack, you're something else, you know that." Tracy sighed. Jack looked hard at Tracy. He saw the stress, the worry, the fear and the confusion written across her exhausted face.

"Tracy," Jack said calmly. Tracy looked at him.

"I have to tell you something." He said. Tracy raised her brows.

"I'm an Angel."

"Huh?"

"I'm an Angel." He repeated. "You know wings, halo, white robes, and good friends with the Big Man upstairs?" Tracy stood with a blank face, not knowing if he was serious or yanking her chain.

"You have an unusual sense of humor."

"I'm not being funny." Jack said. Tracy shook her head and smiled.

"Ok if, you're an Angel where are your wings, why can't you fly?" She asked.

"When God sends us down to Earth, he wraps us in flesh, so we seem human to everyone. You know, just how Jesus was." Tracy laughed.

"Why'd he sent you?"

"You called on him." Jack said. "Remember? The night you went to the graveyard to visit your father? You asked for help, and He sent me."

The color drained from Tracy's face.

"How do you know that? About me? About my father?"

"I know this is hard to believe Tracy but it's true. I know your father. Jackson Nimrod, he's a really nice guy, used to be a policeman right, it's a shame how he went." Tracy shook her head.

"Where do you come up with these things?"

"What? You think I'm lying about this, I don't lie. I know the truth and now so do you. I am an angel."

"Stop it." Tracy snapped. "This isn't a joke." At that moment the door swung open. Jeremiah stood clutching his mother's hand, tears streaming down her face. She walked over to bed and grabbed Jack's hand, smiling.

"Thank you," she said, "so much. I don't know what I'd do without my son."

"You are welcome but just thank God that I was there." Jack replied.

"Oh I will." She stated, letting go of his hand and turning to leave, Jeremiah trailing behind her. Tracy took one last glance at Jack, as a random gust of air came through, and followed her family out.

Chapter 24

And ye shall seek me, and find me, when ye shall search for me with all your heart.

-Jeremiah 29:13

Sirens blared. Red lights flashed. Nurses and doctors scattered. Tracy jolted forward from the hospital waiting room chair; heart beating, head racing. Something was very wrong. A nurse ran up the hall to the receptionist's desk.

"He's gone." She cried.

"What?" The receptionist replied.

"You know the one who got shot, the lucky one, Jack." The nurse repeated. "He's gone." The receptionist jumped on the phone, quickly dialing.

"Code Red. We have a missing patient." She called into the receiver. "I repeat Code Red!" Tracy got on her feet and quickly ran down the hall in disbelief.

"Oh God, what is going on?" She thought, picking up her pace, passing by frazzled nurses and mumbling doctors. Tracy reached the room and shoved the door open. He *was* gone. The bed was empty, nothing but wrinkled sheets. Tubes and IV's tossed to the floor, leaking, forming a clear, odorous puddle. She looked at the heart monitor; it beeped as it read unresponsive. Tracy was at a loss of breath. She backed away but stopped when she felt a firm hand on her shoulder. She turned around and stumbled, falling backwards at the sight.

"Wha-" She began, evading as the figure bent down, kneeling in front of her.

"Jack." She whispered. He smiled. Tracy closed her eyes, shaking her head. She opened them once more and gazed upon the figures face; bald head, thin, graying beard and sharp, deep brown eyes.

"Daddy?" she gasped, as her eyes filled with tears. The figure didn't say a word. He lifted his hand. Tracy stared at the gold cross that hung from a dainty gold chain. Suddenly footsteps were heard coming toward the room. The figures smile disappeared. Tracy blinked and he was gone. Tracy sat motionless, breathless and in aw, the chain resting on the floor in front of her. A random gust of air came through. Tracy grabbed the chain and stood up. She took a look around the empty room, confused but yet not completely out of the loop. A nurse walked in seeing Tracy and motioned for her to follow her up the hall. Tracy looked at the chain and slowly clipped it around her neck. She nodded to the nurse and began to trail behind her. Tracy stopped, feeling a chill and turned back one last time. Jack stood at the Heart Monitor, smiling. Tracy blinked and he was gone. She stared at the Heart Monitor, watching the thin line roll straight across the screen. For a moment Tracy could have sworn she saw the line go jagged and slowly fall back into place. A random gust of air came through, wrapping its self around her. Tracy smiled and listened; a soft whisper. "I love you." A tear rolled down her face, knowing it was neither Jack, nor her father, but someone even greater, who was speaking. Tracy sighed and reached her hand up toward her neck, fingering her chain. She turned and walked out of the room, closing the door tightly behind her.

Then Peter said unto them, Repent and be baptized every one of you in the name of Jesus Christ for the remission of sins, and ye shall receive the Gift of the Holy Ghost.

-Acts 2:38

And they were all filled with the Holy Ghost, and began to speak with other tongues, as the Spirit gave them utterance.

-Acts 2:4